Dear Parent:

Congratulations! Your child is taking the first steps on an exciting journey. The destination? Independent reading!

STEP INTO READING® will help your child get there. The program offers five steps to reading success. Each step includes fun stories and colorful art. There are also Step into Reading Sticker Books, Step into Reading Math Readers, Step into Reading Write-In Readers, Step into Reading Phonics Readers, and Step into Reading Phonics First Steps! Boxed Sets—a complete literacy program with something for every child.

Learning to Read, Step by Step!

Ready to Read Preschool–Kindergarten
• big type and easy words • rhyme and rhythm • picture clues
For children who know the alphabet and are eager to begin reading.

Reading with Help Preschool–Grade 1
• basic vocabulary • short sentences • simple stories
For children who recognize familiar words and sound out new words with help.

Reading on Your Own Grades 1–3
• engaging characters • easy-to-follow plots • popular topics
For children who are ready to read on their own.

Reading Paragraphs Grades 2–3
• challenging vocabulary • short paragraphs • exciting stories
For newly independent readers who read simple sentences with confidence.

Ready for Chapters Grades 2–4
• chapters • longer paragraphs • full-color art
For children who want to take the plunge into chapter books but still like colorful pictures.

STEP INTO READING® is designed to give every child a successful reading experience. The grade levels are only guides. Children can progress through the steps at their own speed, developing confidence in their reading, no matter what their grade.

Remember, a lifetime love of reading starts with a single step!

For Ramona and her buddies

Published in the United States by Random House Children's Books, a division of Random House, Inc., New York, in conjunction with Disney Enterprises, Inc.

www.stepintoreading.com

www.randomhouse.com/kids/disney

Educators and librarians, for a variety of teaching tools, visit us at
www.randomhouse.com/teachers

Library of Congress Cataloging-in-Publication Data
Jordan, Apple.
Driving buddies / by Apple Jordan; illustrated by Disney Storybook Artists.
p. cm. — (Step into reading. Step 2 book)
Summary: On the way to the big race, a racecar named Lightning McQueen gets lost but he manages to make new friends and learn what is truly important in life.
ISBN-13: 978-0-7364-2339-7 (trade)
ISBN-10: 0-7364-2339-7 (trade)
ISBN-13: 978-0-7364-8043-7 (lib. bdg.)
ISBN-10: 0-7364-8043-9 (lib. bdg.)
[1. Friendship—Fiction. 2. Racing—Fiction. 3. Automobiles—Fiction.]
PZ7.J755 Dri 2006 [E]—dc22 2005022618

Printed in the United States of America   15 14 13   First Edition

DISNEY · PIXAR
Cars

Driving Buddies

adapted by Apple Jordan

illustrated by the Disney Storybook Artists

Inspired by the art and character designs created by Pixar Animation Studios

Random House 🏠 New York

McQueen was

a race car.

He was shiny and fast.

He wanted one thing—
to win the big race!

Mater was a tow truck.
He was old and rusty.
He wanted one thing—
a best friend.

Mater lived
in a little town.
The streets were quiet.
All was calm.

One night,
McQueen got lost
on his way
to the big race.

He sped into
the little town.
Sheriff chased him.
McQueen got scared!

He flew into fences!

He crashed into cones!

He ripped up the road!

He made a big mess.

McQueen was
sent to jail.
He met Mater there.
Mater liked
McQueen right away.

Sally, the town lawyer,
and the other cars
wanted McQueen
to fix the road.

McQueen could not
leave town until
the job was done.

McQueen got to work.

He was unhappy.

Mater wanted

to show him some fun.

He took McQueen
tractor tipping.
It <u>was</u> fun.

McQueen told Mater
why he wanted
to win the big race.

He would have fame
and a new look.
He would be a winner!

Mater was happy.

He had

a new best friend.

McQueen fixed
the road at last!
The news reporters
found McQueen!

Mack the truck
was glad to see him!
It was time to go
to the big race.

Mater was sad
to see his buddy leave.
The other cars
were sad, too.

So Mater and his friends
went to the racetrack.
They helped McQueen.

But McQueen still
did not win.
He helped an old friend
finish the race instead.

Now he knew
that winning was not
what he wanted most.

What he wanted most
were friends.